THE ESSENTIAL SONGWRITER'S CONTRACT HANDBOOK

Published by

N S A I

Nashville Songwriters Association International
15 Music Square West
Nashville, Tennessee 37203
USA
1994

CONTENTS

PREFACE

What is it that motivates the songwriter to create? The need for expression through music and lyric, the gratification of a completed work, the camaraderie of artistic and musical interaction, the satisfaction of the ego, hearing the work on the radio or on an album, the thrill of reaching the masses and possibly seeing a work become, in some way, representative of the culture. . . Surely, these are all motivations which songwriters and artists, in general, might share. Songwriting is fun.

Rarely would songwriters list copyright ownership or royalty accounting as motivations. They are part of the mundane business world. Copyright administration is tedious, complicated, not fun. Leave it to the music publishers... and music publishers have been all too happy to oblige. In most cases, they receive 50 percent of a song's earnings for their services. For the opportunity to indulge their art and relinquish the responsibility of marketing and administration, songwriters have been obliging as well, content to let music publishers define the rules and percentages. That is, until the songs become hits, the money going to the publisher becomes substantial, and the songwriter realizes he/she is no longer the owner nor controller of the work... Street Education 101!

On a morning in May 1992, the *Nashville Songwriters Association International* (NSAI) Pro Steering Committee was hosting a two-hour meeting at the Vanderbilt Plaza Hotel to promote the relatively new Professional Membership Division (Pro Division).

The meeting was a well attended affair by many of Nashville's most successful songwriters, who thought it wonderful that the Pro Membership Division existed and that it was able to coordinate, for the first time, a unified presence on behalf of NSAI members. The program featured a panel of four respected NSAI writers, who attended the Washington, DC legislative conferences. They reviewed the legislative proceedings and discussed issues relevant to NSAI. Everyone recognized these as important issues.

An hour-and-a-half into the meeting, it became apparent to me that one of the most fundamental and significant areas of day-to-day songwriter life was going unmentioned. For that matter, I am not sure it had even been considered. I remember raising my hand to ask a question thinking that it was so off the topic at hand that perhaps it would be dismissed by the panel. It was, *We've discussed all that is being done to protect our rights on the national level, but the concern I hear most often expressed by songwriters on a daily basis is their relationship with their publishers... the fact that publishers have such vast catalogs, yet such a low ratio of songpluggers... that a songwriter's songs are largely forgotten once the writer is no longer active with a publisher... that contractually the songwriter is bound and obligated by so much, yet the publisher is usually obligated to nothing more than the vague term 'best efforts.' Isn't the songwriter-publisher relationship one of the most important matters that the Pro Membership Division could address?*

I was surprised by a spontaneous round of applause and knew immediately that I had hit a nerve. The thoughts expressed in my question became the topic of discussion for the rest of the meeting and out into the hall. It wasn't publisher bashing. It was a release of the frustration that every experienced songwriter had felt at one time or another. The relationship between writer and publisher had historically been slanted toward the publisher for too long and inevitably led to a feeling of inequity by many a songwriter. At the conclusion of the meeting, voice after voice asked, *What can we do?*

It was at this moment that the **NSAI Equity Committee** was born to set the framework for a more equitable business environment for songwriters. The next question was how best to go about developing the framework. Forming the Committee was no problem. Virtually every professional writer contacted welcomed the opportunity to contribute, and contribute they did. The first few meetings were think tanks. *Do we draft a sample contract? Do we set up an* *information hotline? Do we meet with publishers? Do we establish a consultation panel of attorneys to counsel individual members?* You are holding what in consensus was felt to be the best solution--a **handbook** that will walk the songwriter through what ultimately is the definition of his/her relationship with a publisher, the *Publishing Agreement.*

Songwriters often enter into publishing agreements based largely on their personal relationship with a songplugger or other individual at the company, but the experienced songwriter knows that staff personnel get promoted or fired; they move on to other companies or even die. The personal equation is important; but, in the end, the songwriter is both bound and protected by what is contained in the publishing agreement, and knows that the agreement is usually binding for a great many years.

The songwriter-publisher relationship can be an extremely lucrative and mutually rewarding one. However, in any business negotiation, the party issuing the agreement typically words such an agreement to his/her own advantage. Since the words almost always emanate from the publisher, publishing agreements have over the years distilled the essence of what is to the publisher's advantage.

This book should, in no way, be regarded as trying to denigrate the value of an effective and honest publisher. Our effort here is to define the workings, explain the intent, and expand the boundaries, aiming at the final agreement that is equitable to both parties. Remember, everything is negotiable, and it should be. An informed, educated songwriting community creates a more equitable business environment for everyone. The chance becomes greater for songwriters at every level to get a more fair deal than perhaps would have been available in the past. At least, that is our goal and I hope we have met it.

We call this a **handbook** because it is not so much intended to be read from cover to cover as it is to be used as a reference work. The Committee is proud of its efforts. We believe they are unique. We have tried extremely hard to be thorough. We also feel certain that, when it comes time to negotiate or renegotiate a publishing agreement, songwriters at every level will benefit from the wisdom contained here.

What makes this handbook unique is that it is written by professional songwriters, writers who have written many hit songs and entered into many publishing agreements; and by one great friend of writers who co-owns a successful independent publishing firm and produces records.

This group is privy to what other successful songwriters with whom they associate and work are agreeing in publishing agreements. They discuss what is possible. . . what is progressive. . . what is theoretical. . . Street Education 201, if you will!

The Equity Committee members (pp. xv & 103) chose which chapters they preferred to write and you will find a variety of styles from one to the next. No one was compensated for time or effort. All have attended countless meetings and written this handbook because they felt the cause was just and the need was great. For this and more, each member deserves a special *thanks!*

There are a few other individuals who were instrumental in creating this handbook. *Pat Rogers,* Executive Director of NSAI, championed the cause from the beginning. *Sara Light* of NSAI probably has more hours in this book than anyone, entering and re-entering the many revisions on computer and coordinating our diverse group of contributors. Songwriters *Peter McCann* and *Sam Lorber* and attorney *John Beiter*, though not actual members of the Committee, contributed several chapters. *Brownlee Ferguson* and *Richard Perna*, both experienced independent publishers, shared freely of their knowledge in licensing and in foreign royalties. *Connie Lord* gave graciously of her time and expertise to edit our rough-hewn work into actual book form. The *attorney review panel* (p. xvii), consisting of various noted entertainment attorneys, was given specific chapters to critique. The attorneys' comments were duly noted; some were incorporated and some were disputed, but all were enlightening and greatly appreciated. Everyone of these individuals merits a ***very special thanks*** from the Committee.

One more person must be thanked. Without a doubt, the most important effort on this project came from a very unique individual, my Committee Cochair, *Dennis Lord*. Dennis has brought to bear both his practical experience as a successful songwriter and the depth of his training and practice as an entertainment attorney to guide the project where it needed to go. He gave a great amount of his time unselfishly to editing and coordinating this handbook and he deserves much of the credit for its completion. It was Dennis' energy and follow-through that, ultimately, got the job done.

Lewis Anderson
Nashville, Tennessee

THE NSAI EQUITY COMMITTEE

The NSAI Equity Committee members are

- *Lewis Anderson*, Cochair

- *Dennis Lord*, Cochair

- *Michael Clark*

- *Steve Dean*

- *Gene Nelson*

- *Lisa Palas*

- *Will Robinson*

- *Jim Rooney*

- *Jim Rushing*

- *Karen Staley*

Each member listed contributed at least one chapter to *The Essential Songwriter's Contract Handbook*. Some wrote more than one chapter; all submitted editorial critiques on handbook sections. Other comments and analyses were evaluated during the Committee's numerous think-tank sessions.

For an informal introduction to the NSAI Equity Committee members see APPENDIX *A*, Page 103. ♪

ATTORNEY REVIEWERS

The NSAI Equity Committee expresses sincere appreciation to a number of attorneys from around the country who selflessly reviewed handbook chapter(s) and offered pertinent critiques and commentaries. Some commentaries were included verbatim; some were paraphrased. All reviewers influenced the final outcome of the handbook.

In special recognition of the attorney reviewers' contributions, they are noted here in alphabetical listing per contributing attorney.

- *JOHN C. BEITER*
  Neal & Harwell
  Nashville, Tennessee

- *DOROTHY K. CAMPBELL-BELL*
  Counsel
  Word Record & Music Group
  Nashville, Tennessee

- *RICHARD H. FRANK, Jr.*
  Nashville, Tennessee

- *J. RUSH HICKS, Jr.*
  Maddox & Hicks
  Nashville, Tennessee

- *MARY PATY LYNN JETTON*
  Manier, Herod, Hollabaugh & Smith
  Nashville, Tennessee

- *RUSSEL A. JONES, Jr.*
  Gordon, Martin & Jones
  Nashville, Tennessee

- *PHILIP K. LYON*
  Jack, Lyon & Jones, P.A.
  Nashville, Tennessee
  and
  Little Rock, Arkansas

- *DAVID L. MADDOX*
  Maddox & Hicks
  Nashville, Tennessee

- *MALCOLM MIMMS*
  Loeb & Loeb
  Nashville, Tennessee

- *W. MICHAEL MILOM*
  Wyatt, Tarrant & Coombs
  Nashville, Tennessee

- *STEPHEN K. RUSH*
  The Sukin Law Firm
  New York, New York
  and
  Nashville, Tennessee

- *ALFRED W. SCHLESINGER*
  Schlesinger, Herschman, Marcus & Dave
  Hollywood, California

- *MICHAEL SUKIN*
  The Sukin Law Firm
  New York, New York
  and
  Nashville, Tennessee

- *KATHERINE E. WOODS*
  Jack, Lyon & Jones, P.A.
  Nashville, Tennessee

It is important to note that, ***even though each attorney was requested to review one to three chapters, opinions and other material included in this handbook are not necessarily endorsed by the attorney reviewers.*** ♪

INTRODUCTION

The *Nashville Songwriters Association International* (NSAI) Equity Committee members are pleased to provide *The Essential Songwriter's Contract Handbook* for use by interested songwriters on a nationwide basis. It addresses virtually every major area of negotiation covered in songwriter-publisher agreements, as well as informational material not normally found in agreements. Chapters were arranged to coincide, as closely as possible, with their general order of appearance in a *Publishing Agreement.*

Though the songwriters who wrote the chapters, the attorneys who reviewed them, and the many editors who edited them have attempted to develop the handbook as a comprehensive document, the Committee has concluded that each songwriter's publishing agreement is uniquely applicable to a specific songwriter-publisher relationship. While the handbook is intended to function as a songwriter's guide to agreement negotiations and, as such, provides relevant information in general terms, it is strongly recommended that the songwriter consult with his/her attorney on specifics surfacing in each situation. ♪

I. MORAL RIGHTS

CONCEPT

In my initial research to gain some understanding of the term *moral rights* so that I might pass that understanding on to you, I made the assumption that the term was embedded in American Law. I mean, *how is it possible not to have something set in stone concerning a topic with this kind of lofty heading?* Surely, there was some specific body of law on this very subject. Well, *yes* and *no*. *Yes*, the concept does exist and, to some degree, it is acted upon as part of our system of law; and *no*, it is not specifically spelled out if you are a composer and/or lyricist.

The *moral-rights* origins are European, historically Roman, and they reflect an early appreciation of the fact that the work of the artist is inseparable from the artist's soul. The work is an extension of the creator, a representation of the person's inner spirit and vision and, therefore, as much a part of the artist as his arm or mind. It is a projection of the artist's personality and, as such, beyond and separate from the *rights of ownership*. By some, these *rights* are considered *inalienable* regardless of ownership.

America's early brush with the concept of *moral rights* resulted in the *copyright law* that protected the music publisher's monopolistic rights to print. This law was derived from the English copyright law which was really created to protect the economic rights of book publishers rather than the creative rights of authors. The monopoly or exclusive printing right was merely the tool or method used to protect these rights--not exactly a sterling example of higher thinking but, historically, not surprising either. To be fair, where modern American law shies away from speaking directly on this subject, it does supply similar protection under copyright or under conventional labels, such as *unfair competition, defamation, invasion of privacy*, or *breach of contract*.

RIGHT OF ATTRIBUTION
and
RIGHT OF INTEGRITY

So, *what exactly are moral rights, and why should you, the songwriter, even want to know?* By definition, *moral rights* fall into two basic categories, the *right of attribution* and the *right of integrity*.

The *right of attribution* concerns the

- right of the creator to be known as the author of his/her work;

- right to prevent others from being named as the author of his/her work; and the

- right to prevent others from falsely attributing to him/her the authorship of work which the author has not, in fact, written.

The *right of integrity* concerns the

- right to prevent others from making deforming changes in the author's work;

- right to withdraw a published work from distribution if it no longer represents the views of the author; and the

- right to prevent others from using the work or the author's name in such a way as to damage his/her professional standing.

Think about this for a minute. Have a cup of coffee and let this settle into your mind. *Does this give you, the songwriter, a little different slant on your work and career?* It should. The discussion and acknowledged existence of these *rights* should remind you that, while a publisher may invest money in the early stages of your career, you are investing yourself and you are literally a part of what you create. And, because of this fact, you cannot be separated nor should anyone have the right to separate you from your work by denying public attribution to you when your work is presented.

It's reasonable to expect **published credit** for your songs when they are presented on a recording. However, in today's world, it doesn't always happen. It's your words, your music. Yet, everybody from the singer's favorite hairdresser to his/her personal faith healer is credited on the recording, but **no songwriter's credits**! It affects your personal and professional reputation, as well as your financial well-being.

Let's talk about the second major category of rights, the **right of integrity**. Let me give you an example of how bad it can get in a contract. Read the following excerpt all the way through. It is taken from a proposed publishing agreement. I do not know if the songwriter in question signed this contract. Let's hope not.

EXCERPT A
> *Writer expressly acknowledges and agrees that*
> (i)   *Writer's services to be rendered and the rights in musical compositions granted to Publisher under this agreement are of **SPECIAL, UNIQUE, AND INTELLECTUAL CHARACTER** which gives them **PECULIAR VALUE;***
> (ii)   *in the event of Writer's breach of any term, condition, covenant, warranty or*

> *representation of this agreement, Publisher shall be caused irreparable harm for which the remedy at law is inadequate;*
>
> *(iii)*   *Publisher shall be entitled to preliminary and permanent injunctive relief (mandatory or otherwise).*

Time out for a minute. I capitalized those areas of the above excerpt for a reason. This kind of language is not there by accident. You **are *SPECIAL, UNIQUE*,** and *of VALUE.* Your services are something special. They are not asking you to flip burgers. They want to participate in the fruits of your *talent.* The above excerpt is appropriate in defining how important and unique your services are, and it serves an important legal purpose. Excerpt A is not the problem. It merely establishes your position. What follows **is** the problem.

Let's read on. By the way, the French expressions *droit moral* and *droit d'auteur* refer to *moral rights*.

EXCERPT B

> *Writer hereby waives the benefits of any provision of law known as the 'droit moral' or 'droit d'auteur' and the benefits of any similar law of any country of the world. Writer further agrees not to institute, support, maintain or permit any claim, proceeding, action or lawsuit anywhere in the world on the ground any publication or other use by Publisher or*

*its assignees of licensees, including the full exercise of rights under this agreement, in any way constitutes an infringement or violation of any of Writer's droit moral, droit d'auteur or similar right or is in any way a defamation or mutilation of any Musical Composition or part thereof or contains unauthorized variations of the Musical Compositions. If, despite the provisions of the immediately preceding sentence, such a proceeding and/or lawsuit is instituted, Writer specifically **WAIVES HIS OR HER RIGHT TO ANY EQUITABLE RELIEF** including injunction, and any claim to monetary damages; Writer's sole remedy and recourse for the alleged infringements and violations **SHALL BE TO REQUIRE THE REMOVAL OF THE WRITER'S NAME FROM ALL CREDITS, ADVERTISING OR PUBLICITY OF OR RELATING TO ANY SUCH VERSION OF THE MUSICAL COMPOSITION IN QUESTION.***

Is this a piece of business or what? First, you are a unique talent. Next, you have absolutely *no rights* if your potential publisher does major surgery to your work, except, of course, the right to have your name removed from your work if you disagree with the publisher's actions! The publisher could have your song rewritten without your approval and, for that matter, without even notifying you if you signed away your rights as they are presented in the above contract excerpt.

We could go into greater depth but, really, the purpose of all this is to highlight the definition of *moral rights* and to increase your awareness of this subject.

What I'd like to leave you with is this: *An entire industry is built upon your particular talents.* From the highest paid record company executive to the janitor who cleans the building that your publisher calls home, and all in between, *I repeat ALL, rely upon you and all working composers and lyricists to provide the basis for their living.*

They don't like to admit it and they don't like to pay for it, as witnessed by the legal battles over the years regarding royalty payments. But, regardless of their attitude, you should never forget this simple fact. *Under the heading of MORAL RIGHTS lies a bedrock of thought and philosophy which supports the uniqueness of your position as a creator in the arts.* How your potential publisher deals with this area of your contract may speak volumes as to the *type of partner the publisher will be and the type of support mechanism the publisher will offer over the years of your association.*

For a separate but related discussion of your unique services, see *CHAPTER XVI. LIMITATIONS OF PUBLISHER'S USE OF COPYRIGHT*, Page 78, and *CHAPTER XIX. BREACH OF CONTRACT*, Page 93. ♪

II. GRANT OF RIGHTS

Generally, the **grant of rights clause** language appears in the first section of your *Exclusive Songwriters Agreement* or *Single Song Contract*, which grants all or part of the ownership interest in your songs to your publisher. Ownership interest is represented by the **copyright**. Often that contract language reads something like this:

> *Songwriter hereby assigns all rights, title and interests of any nature or kind whatsoever, whether now in existence or hereafter to come into existence, in the Compositions to Publisher, its successors and assigns, together with all copyrights therein, including all renewals, extensions, and reversions thereof.*

The section goes on to cover in detail the rights to your songs which you are relinquishing to a publisher. But, the essence of granting of rights is quoted in the paragraph above.

Let us try this analogy to help clarify the language of the contract. If your song, let's say, is a 1959 pink Cadillac, the *title* to the car is the *copyright*, and the *keys* to the car are the administration rights to your song. When you give the *title* and *keys* to someone else, you cannot do much but sit back and admire the pink Caddy. So it is with the *grant of rights*. You give up the ownership of the song, the right to license its use, the right to collect royalties and, basically, the right to control the song's destiny.

Each portion of this *grant of rights* clause is addressed elsewhere in this book. It will become clearer to you as you read on. But, for the purposes of this chapter, pay attention to this part.

> . . . . . *together with all copyrights, therein,*
> *INCLUDING ALL RENEWALS, EXTENSIONS*
> *AND REVERSIONS THEREOF.*

In your contract negotiation, try to have the *including all renewals, extensions and reversions thereof* deleted from the agreement. Here's why. Since the Copyright Act of 1976 took effect on January 1, 1978, that language has become obsolete and meaningless. You are entitled to reclaim your copyright after approximately 35 years if you give your publisher appropriate notice. It is very possible that the law may change someday. If that language remains in your agreement, you may have given the copyright up for a longer period than necessary.

CHAPTER V. COPYRIGHT OWNERSHIP AND THE WORK-MADE-FOR-HIRE DOCTRINE (p.15) discusses this statutory *right of termination and length of term of copyright.*

By the way, the renewal, extension, and reversion language usually appears several times in your contract, as it does in the short-form copyright assignment which you usually sign for each individual song you write. Delete it everywhere you find it. Of course, it is up to you as to whether or not to put a priority on deleting this language. Follow your instincts and the advice of your attorney. ♪

III. TERM OF DEAL

In fairness to both the songwriter and the publisher, the initial **term** of an *Exclusive Songwriters Agreement* should be no less than *1 year*. It is reasonable to expect a publisher to ask for at least one *1-year option*, and often the publisher will ask for more than one.

Think seriously before agreeing to a contract of more than 3 years. Generally, it is structured as a 1-year agreement with two 1-year options. Assuming that you achieve a good deal of success within these 3 years, an extra 1-year option or two, negotiated at the beginning of your contract, would more than likely not compensate you adequately because your value to the publisher would have increased.

After a 3-year period with the same publisher, it is preferable to negotiate an entirely new contract. You may also consider asking for an increase in your weekly advance, or a draw with each option in anticipation of career growth or in anticipation of being the next *Don Schlitz!* See also *CHAPTER VIII.* **ADVANCES AND RECOUPMENT**, Page 30.

Although you may ask for a 1-year contract with no options, do not let options frighten you because, if you decide you want to leave the publisher, many of them will not force you to stay. On the other hand, if you have contractually agreed to options or to anything else for that matter, **you may be held to it.** Of course, you can ask for a songwriter's option, but consider your position before you use up too much bargaining power to attain it.

Asking a publisher to earn options has, to date, been rare. But, do not preclude the possibility. Whether you are an advanced or entry-level songwriter taking no advance, try to get a clause in your contract which requires the publisher to

> *earn options based on the number of songs cut, the amount of songwriter income earned or, **in lieu** of either of those, an amount of money to purchase the option.*

If you have an even better idea, **by all means, use it.** ♪

IV. EXCLUSIVITY

Exclusivity in a songwriter's contract means that *you can only write for one publisher*, the one with whom you have a signed contract. Any music or lyric written during the term of the contract belongs to the publisher and/or to you, provided you have a *Copublishing Agreement*. Generally, this applies to all forms of music and includes **commercial music, gospel, children's music, commercials**, or **motion pictures**.

It is reasonable for the publisher to expect exclusivity. However, exceptions are possible. For example, if you are a *country-music* songwriter writing for a *country-music* publisher, but you occasionally write *children's music* and get it recorded through your own efforts, you may agree with your publisher to have the children's music **specifically** excluded from your contract. Or, you may negotiate a separate agreement--i.e., a *Copublishing Agreement*.

In any case, try to negotiate a fair and equitable arrangement. Remember, however, that your publisher **also** deserves a fair portion of income from music created during your contract with him/her, especially if he/she is paying you an advance. ♪

V. COPYRIGHT OWNERSHIP AND THE WORK-MADE-FOR-HIRE DOCTRINE

COPYRIGHT OWNERSHIP

Under copyright laws, the **author** of a work is its **owner** and, initially, he/she possesses the **exclusive rights** to control, exploit, and receive payment for use of the work. Surprisingly, the **creator** of a work--e.g., the composer of a song--is not always considered its author. In fact, depending upon the nature of the relationship between them, it may well be that the music **publisher** and not the **songwriter** is considered the author of a song for **copyright** purposes.

Why is this of significance to the songwriter? If the songwriter is the author and he/she enters a contract transferring rights in the composition to a music publisher, the songwriter generally can terminate that transfer and get the song back after 35 years. This **termination right** is a valuable asset that the songwriter will want to retain, especially in the case of a song that goes on to gain wide popularity and has the potential to create substantial income well into the future.

Moreover, the identity of the author directly determines the length of time that copyright protection will be afforded to the song. On the one hand, if the publisher is the author of the composition, the copyright generally will continue for either 75 years from the date of publication or 100 years from the date of creation, whichever period is shorter. On the other hand, if the songwriter is the author, copyright protection in the composition generally will continue for the life of the songwriter or, if there is more than one, for the life of the longest living songwriter plus 50 years.

WORK MADE FOR HIRE

What can a songwriter do to insure that he/she retains the status of author of the composition and, thus, the exclusive rights to exploit it? The most important thing to remember is that the *authorship* of the composition ultimately is determined by the legal relationship between you and the publisher. As a general rule, if you write a composition as an *employee* of the publisher within the scope of that employment, the song is considered a *work made for hire* and the publisher rather than the songwriter is the author. On the other hand, if you are not an employee of the publisher, but merely a so-called *independent contractor*, the composition's authorship remains with the songwriter.

What factors determine whether a songwriter is an employee of the publisher and thus has no authorship status for compositions written in the course of that relationship? The obvious first place to look is the contract itself. Many publishers attempt to include a provision in the contract stating that the publisher *hereby employs* the songwriter and the songwriter *hereby accepts employment* with the publisher so that the publisher will be considered the author and therefore owner of compositions written under the contract, and the songwriter will have no termination right in the songs. One wonders how many songwriters have signed contracts accepting employment with publishers without understanding what they may be giving up in the process.

Significantly, however, although the contract language offers some evidence of the nature of the relationship, it is not alone sufficient to create an **employer-employee relationship** between the songwriter and the publisher. Other factors must be considered. In the 1989 landmark case of *Community For Creative Non-Violence v. Reid*, the Supreme Court ruled that, in determining whether the creator of a work is an employee, the crucial factor is whether the person doing the hiring, such as the song publisher, has the **right to control the manner and means by which the product is accomplished.** The Court noted that the following considerations, among others, are relevant:

- skill required to create the work;

- source of the instruments and tools used to create the work;

- length of the relationship between the parties;

- whether the hiring party has the right to assign additional projects to the hired party;

- extent of the hired party's discretion over when and how long to work;

- method of payment; and

- hired party's role in hiring and paying assistants.

Looking at these factors, it appears that, if you

- use the publisher's musical instruments and/or demo studio,

- have a longstanding relationship with the publisher,

- receive weekly or monthly payments,

- are restricted as to the cowriters with whom you can work,

- are expected to write a certain quota of songs per month or year, and

- receive any typical employee benefits,

you might be considered an *employee* and the publisher might be considered the *author* and owner of songs *made for hire* under the contract.

On the other hand, if, as a recently signed songwriter, you

- use your own musical instruments and demo studio,

- are subject to no quota or cowriter restrictions, and

- receive no regular payments or traditional employee benefits,

it is more likely that you will be considered an *independent contractor* and will retain the authorship status of the compositions.

In the final analysis, the more the songwriter-publisher relationship resembles a traditional employer-employee relationship, the more the publisher is likely to be considered the author of the songs. In the employer-employee relationship, points to remember are as follows.

- Because the contract is an obvious first place to look to determine the nature of the relationship, the songwriter should avoid the typical *employment* language in publishing contracts.

- Except in the area of television and movies, the standard songwriter contract typically does not create

19

an employment relationship that would render the subject songs *works made for hire.*

- In a narrow sense, the work may be considered a *work made for hire* if it has been specially ordered or commissioned by someone else even if a work's creator is not an employee. ♪

VI. COPYRIGHT OWNERSHIP AND COPUBLISHING

COPYRIGHT OWNERSHIP

The moment a song is created and expressed in some tangible form, it is protected by **copyright**. The owner of the copyright is the songwriter unless he/she has contractually assigned the ownership to another party. This is typically what occurs when a songwriter signs an *Exclusive Songwriters Agreement* and/or a *Single Song Agreement* with a publisher. However, there are many diverse ways to structure a publishing relationship with another party short of giving up full ownership and the rights associated with such ownership.

COPUBLISHING AGREEMENT

In a *Copublishing Agreement*, the songwriter assigns a portion of his/her ownership to another party. A typical copublishing division of ownership is 50-50. Sometimes the percentages may fall to the benefit of one party or the other, as in the 60-40, 75-25, or even the 90-10 divisions.

Usually, the publisher wants total *administrative rights* no matter what percentage of ownership he/she retains. This is an important point to negotiate. If the publisher advances money to the songwriter, the publisher will invariably want the right to administer the entire copyright so as to insure the return of the publisher's investment more effectively. The songwriter who takes no advance is more likely to retain the administrative rights to his/her share of the copyright. The songwriter who does take an advance should try to negotiate a *termination* of the administrative rights to his/her share when the publisher has *recouped* those advances.

Why are the administrative rights so important? They are important because they include the right to assign the copyright at any time, as well as the right to control the *licensing* and *royalty* collection for the song and the right to control the *assignment* of these administrative rights. A songwriter, who does not retain these rights or does not regain them through termination, has contractually given away the business control of his/her song. This way, his/her copyright ownership becomes a future stream of income only, payable through the owner of the administrative rights. Should the songwriter wish to sell his/her share of the copyright in the future, the value of that share is greatly enhanced if the administrative rights come with it and it is diminished if they do not.

A publisher may also ask for an additional **administrative fee** in the range of from 5 to 20 percent of the gross royalties to cover the cost of providing these licensing and accounting services. In essence, this increases the publisher's share of income substantially. **Administrative fees should be reduced or eliminated from the contract if possible** (*CHAPTER VII. ADMINISTRATION*, p. 25).

If you, the songwriter, are required to assign 100 percent of a song to your publisher, it is usually because you have not established a successful track record as a hit songwriter or, possibly, because you are asking for a large advance. Whatever the reason, **it is in your best interest to try to establish a point at which you may become a part owner of copyrights contractually assigned**. Your publisher may resist this for works under the initial term, but may consent to copublishing in future option periods. Copublishing could also be contingent upon certain levels of achievement, such as recoupment of advances or a set amount of royalties earned, record sales, or chart position.

Your publisher may resist copublishing and offer instead a form of **income participation**. This means that you would be entitled to receive a percentage of your publisher's net income, usually after deduction of all expenses, but would not share in copyright ownership and all the rights that go with it. **Income participation is not copyright ownership**.

For works that are **not** works for hire, the term of copyright lasts through the life of the last surviving cowriter of the song plus 50 years. If you never assign the copyright, you are the **owner for life**, and your heirs for the rest of the term. A typical assignment to a publisher is for the entire term unless the songwriter or the songwriter's heirs exercise a right under copyright law to reclaim the song's copyright ownership between the 35th and 40th year of assignment. This is different from the contractual reversion discussed in *CHAPTER V. COPYRIGHT OWNERSHIP AND THE WORK-FOR-HIRE DOCTRINE*, Page 15.

You may limit the term of assignment by contract. In this event, the **publisher's interest in the copyright would expire at a determined time as stated in the contract**. If the publisher pays for this assignment, this embodies a **leasing** arrangement where the publisher leases an interest in the copyright for a specified length of time. If the money paid for this interest is considered an advance, the publisher may request that the term of the lease be extended automatically until all the money is recouped. ♪

VII. ADMINISTRATION

RESPONSIBILITIES

The songwriter of a musical composition is also its *copyright owner and publisher* unless that right is granted to another. As copyright owner, it is possible to grant *rights of administration* to another. Administration is essentially the nuts and bolts of publishing. The administrator

- has the right to execute *licenses* and *contracts* relating to the composition, and

- is empowered to collect the proceeds flowing from them in all fields of use within the territory covered by the agreement for the term of the agreement.

The contract will specify such things as *mechanical, synchronization, audiovisual, performance,* and *printed-matter rights*, and should also cover *future technologies* by language, such as

> *all other rights and usages of the composition now known or hereafter coming into existence.*

An *Administration Agreement*, or the part of a songwriter agreement that pertains to administration, will specify that the administrator will

- register *claims to copyright*, as well as renewals if applicable;

- act as *agent for collection* for the publisher and, as such, accept *royalty statements* and all *accounting* relating to the composition, and collect all *monies, royalties, advances,* or other compensation accruing to the composition;

- negotiate all *contracts* and *licenses* pertaining to the composition; and

- clear the songs with the appropriate performing rights societies.

The performance of these duties requires that the administrator become the *exclusive agent* and *special attorney-in-fact* for the publisher. Accordingly, the administrator

- executes contracts,

- handles and accounts for all monies accrued by the composition, and

- renders an accounting of all income and expenses, excluding ordinary secretarial, clerical, and general overhead expenses, such as fees paid to collection agents and subpublishers.

With regard to the administration of **mechanical rights**, it is possible to require that the collection agency selected, such as *Harry Fox, Copyright Management, Inc. (CMI),* or some other, be mutually agreed upon. With respect to subpublishing or collection in territories other than the United States, it may also be desirable to agree mutually either to use a subpublisher or to deal directly with the local performing and mechanical rights organizations. Many arrangements are possible and a great deal of flexibility is required.

Accounting for monies is customarily done within 90 days following the end of each calendar half-year. Some administration contracts have quarterly accounting within 30 days. The administrator deducts allowable expenses plus an administrative fee which is negotiable. An amount of 10 percent of the gross income is not uncommon.

ADMINISTRATION AGREEMENT

An *Administration Agreement* typically will define the territory covered as *The World* or as *The Universe* unless otherwise specified. The term of such an agreement is open to negotiation. A typical arrangement these days could be 2 to 5 years, renewable for additional 1-year consecutive periods unless terminated by either party at least 30 days prior to expiration of the current term.

Also included in a typical *Administration Agreement* is a *right for the publisher to examine the books of the administrator.* This right is usually limited to once a year, with 7 days or more written notice (*CHAPTER XIV. ACCOUNTING AND AUDIT*, p. 66). However, the right is exercised all too seldom, but it can provide a valuable opportunity for an accurate understanding of the sources of income for a particular composition and, also, for identifying any problems which may arise in the money-collecting process. Such examination can go a long way toward keeping an administrator responsive to the songwriter's concerns.

For his/her part, the publisher of the composition warrants in the agreement that the *composition is original* and shall not infringe on anyone else's copyright or other rights, and that there are *no suits or claims pending against the composition.* The publisher also agrees that, if any monies are collected by or delivered to the publisher, the publisher shall deliver all such monies to the administrator *promptly*, and that they shall be considered a part of the *gross income* accruing to the composition subject to the administration fee. Also, included in the agreement will be a clause stating that,

*if the administrator settles any suit regarding
a composition, any monetary recovery shall
also be considered gross income and shall be
subject to the administration fee.*

An *Administration Agreement* very often becomes useful to
a songwriter who has accumulated a catalog of songs and
who has been taking care of them himself/herself. If some
of the compositions have been recorded and monies are
flowing from various sources, there can come a time when
it makes sense to engage a competent, honest
administrator to take over the job. Such an arrangement
does not include advances or oblige the administrator to
exploit the compositions in any way. The sole function of
the administrator **will be to insure that all copyrights,
licenses, contracts, etc., are in order, up-to-date, and that
monies owed are properly collected, accounted for, and
distributed.**

For the songwriter who is well established or the
artist/writer who is the primary vehicle for the
composition(s), an *Administration Agreement* affords the
maximum control over the compositions' total ownership
for a very reasonable cost and the security that comes from
knowing that the copyrights are well protected. As always,
an administrator should be examined thoroughly for honesty
and competence.

Discussions *re* administration services are also in *CHAPTER
VI. COPYRIGHT OWNERSHIP AND COPUBLISHING* (p. 21)
and in *CHAPTER IX. ROYALTIES* (p. 40). ♪

VIII.   ADVANCES AND RECOUPMENT

ADVANCES

Advances vary widely. At present in Nashville, an entry-level songwriter can expect something between $150 and $300 per week for the first year of his/her deal. This depends on the size and financial resources of the publisher. Advance amounts may vary in other major music centers depending on cost of living, economics, and expectations.

For more successful songwriters, the sky is the limit. It depends on the skill and imagination that you and your attorney put into it. And, although some may disagree, it may also depend on your relationship with your publisher and your attorney's relationship with your publisher. Now that the money question is answered, let us look at some facts about *advances*.

Types of Advances

Advances are defined as

> *monies paid before an otherwise proper time of payment; money paid in advance to be repaid under certain conditions; money provided on credit; a loan or gift.*

The point is simple. When your publisher gives you an advance, you are not receiving a wage or salary as in traditional occupations. You are, instead, getting money that will be recouped by your publisher later from royalties otherwise due to you from a recorded song or songs.

It is worth noting that, while advances are recoupable, they are generally nonreturnable. So, if you see **nonreturnable** language pertaining to advances in your contract, it probably means that you do not have to pay back any advances made by the publisher from sources of income unrelated to your songwriter-publisher contract or groups of contracts between the same parties. In fact, one attorney who read this chapter commented,

> *Nonreturnable in this context means **nonreturnable under any circumstances**. I have never seen an advance that <u>was</u> returnable.*

There are other forms of advances with which you should be familiar. For instance, if your publisher gives you an **airline ticket** to Montana to write with your favorite cowriter, that could be an advance. And, if your publisher picks up the **hotel bill** while you are there, that could be an advance. Of course, do not forget **per diem**, the daily spending allowance. That could be an advance, too.

Now, if your publisher has *asked* you to go to Montana and write, that should be an investment your publisher is making. In such a case, your publisher should bear the costs and should not charge them back to you; or, at least, split the advance/investment on a 50-50 basis with you. It all depends on what the contract says.

Finally, do not forget that, very often a publisher will consider the *costs of demoing* a song or, at least, some portion of that cost as an advance (*CHAPTER XII. DEMOS*, p. 60). Other items which may be considered advances are

- your share of costs to *hire an independent promoter* to help promote a record, but only if previously specified in your contract or in copublishing situations;

- your share of *legal costs* to defend or settle a lawsuit; and

- *health insurance* for you and/or your family.

To sum up, in most cases, portions of demo costs and any travel expenses you may have will be deducted or recouped from your royalties by your publisher before your publisher writes you a check. You should receive a detailed statement reflecting all deductions or recoupments from your royalties along with your check or, sometimes, *in lieu* of your check. Be sure to review all statements you receive for accuracy.

Here is a word of advice. Advances are not the **end all and be all** of a publishing deal. In fact, they can come back to haunt you. Be careful not to get used to a large advance. The dynamics of the business are such that you may have a couple of **off** years, and a large monthly advance may cost you your deal. As a matter of practicality, consider taking the smallest advance on which you can get by, perhaps enough to keep you from having to take a second job; then wait for the big checks that come with a hit to be your security cushion.

Something else to consider is that, as a general rule, **the larger your advance, the less likely your opportunity to participate in coownership of copyrights to your songs.**

IDEAS FOR THE NINETIES, a later section of this Chapter (p. 36), offers additional information on types of advances and gives some alternatives.

RECOUPMENT

Back to definitions. **Recoupment** means

> *the recovery of a loss by a later gain; holding back something which is otherwise due because there is equitable reason to do so.*

33

In an *Exclusive Songwriters Agreement*, the equitable reason to recoup from a songwriter is that the **publisher advanced the songwriter money**. The publisher recoups that money from royalties otherwise due to the songwriter for so long as the songwriter has an unrecouped balance of advances which he/she has not repaid the publisher.

Recoupment Sources

The publisher's primary recoupment sources are royalties. A detailed discussion of royalty sources is in *CHAPTER IX. ROYALTIES*, Page 40. Royalties are derived from sources, such as

- *mechanical*--i.e., sale of CDs, tapes, etc.;

- *sync licensing*--i.e., use of the song with a video image;

- *foreign*--i.e., sales, performance and other uses;

- *print uses*;

- *DART Royalties* from digital hardware and software; and

- *public performances* of the song.

Typically, the publisher will recoup advances from all royalty sources collected by the publisher on behalf of the songwriter, including mechanical, sync uses, print uses, and others. But, as a general rule, ***performance royalties*** are paid directly to the songwriter by a performing rights society. Therefore, most publishers will not recoup from performance royalties owed to the songwriter.

Assignment of Performance Royalties

There are some publishers who ***do*** insist on an ***assignment of performance royalties*** by you to them so that they may recoup any advances you have received. Generally, ***this practice is not recommended***. And, if a clause requiring assignment of performance royalties to your publisher appears in your contract, consider it a serious stumbling block to a successful relationship with your publisher and do everything possible to have it removed from the contract.

If your publisher insists that your performance royalties be paid to you through him/her, there should be a good reason. The only good reason we can come up with is that the publisher has advanced substantial sums of money to you. We do not mean a couple-hundred bucks a week. We are talking about large sums, which may not be fairly recouped from nonperformance royalties alone. In cases like these, assignment of performance royalties may be reasonable and in order. Use your own judgement.

A publisher might insist on an assignment of performance royalties just to get the ***float***. A float means that a publisher earns interest on songwriter royalty income held in the publisher's bank account until the next date the publisher is required to pay royalties to the songwriter.

In any event, *be sure you are clear on what sources of income your publisher taps to recoup advances.* If the publisher insists on an assignment of performance royalties, be sure it is for a good reason, and *float* is not a good enough reason.

IDEAS FOR THE 90s

There are an infinite number of ways to *structure advances and income* in an *Exclusive Songwriters Agreement.* If you can think of it and it is legal, it *can* be done. Some of the following suggestions may or may not apply to your specific situation. A few may be difficult to get included in your contract right now, but keep persisting. Times change.

Recoupment from a Percentage of Your Songwriter's Share

If you have enough clout, you may want to suggest that your publisher recoup from only a percentage of royalties otherwise due, such as 50 percent. For example, say your publisher has advanced you $200. Along the way, your publisher collects $100 in royalties which would be due to you if there had been no advances. Under most publishing contracts, your publisher would take the entire $100 toward recoupment of advances. In that case, you would receive nothing.

If, however, your publisher is recouping from 50 percent of your share, you would receive $50 of the royalties and your publisher would keep $50 dollars toward advances previously paid to you. This will leave you with a balance of $150 to be paid off. Under this scenario, you would get at least some portion of the royalties and your publisher would recoup a portion of the advances.

Lump-sum Advances from Royalties in the Pipeline

In lieu of a weekly advance, you may want to consider a lump-sum advance based on royalties in the pipeline. For instance, you may negotiate an agreement with your publisher under which your publisher will write you a check for a specified sum if a particular song is recorded and it reaches the top 30 on the *Billboard* or *Radio & Records* charts. An additional sum would be paid if the song reaches the top 20; another if the song reaches the top 10; another if the song reaches the top 5; and, yet, another advance if the song reaches **No. 1.** This gives you more immediate access to dollars that would otherwise be in the pipeline and would not reach you for a period of 9 to 18 months or longer. This formula could be used for quicker payments of both performance and mechanical royalties if it is properly negotiated between you and your publisher. Such a negotiated clause might involve the assignment of your performance royalties to your publisher.

Nonrecoupable Bonuses On Gold/Platinum Records

If you are a songwriter who has had some success, you may propose in your next contract that your publisher pay you a nonrecoupable bonus for each song you have on a record that goes gold, platinum, or multiplatinum. This bonus could be in addition to your percentage of royalties due, and could vary in size from the price of a steak dinner to whatever you and your publisher determine is reasonable.

You can figure out what is reasonable yourself. As of November 1993, the U.S. Copyright Office determined that the statutory rate for mechanical royalties was $0.0661 or 6.61 cents. That 6.61 cents represents the combined total of publisher's and songwriter's shares per song, per record manufactured and distributed. So, at 500,000 units sold, the total mechanical royalty is $33,050. This amount is shared by all the songwriters and publishers associated with a particular song on the basis of their contractually agreed-upon percentages. With the knowledge of the total dollars involved, a songwriter, the songwriter's attorney, and the publisher can figure out together an appropriate nonrecoupable bonus for each 500,000 units sold.

Purchase of Existing Catalog

Sometimes publishers believe that they should be entitled to your existing catalog without having to pay for it. It is fair and reasonable to ask your publisher to *purchase* your existing catalog for some amount of money rather than *advance* money to you for it. The selling price depends on your bargaining position.

Another variation would be to agree that the publisher could earn an *interest* in any of your existing unrecorded songs by obtaining a major label recording of it. (See *CHAPTER XI. EXISTING CATALOG*, p. 58.)

These are just a few of your options. And, even as this book goes to print, there are very specific, new, and innovative contractual relationships developing between songwriters and publishers--relationships that will help change the nature of such agreements and make them equitable for both songwriter and publisher. ♪

IX. ROYALTIES

TYPES OF ROYALTIES

This discussion will review the different types of royalties you, the songwriter, are entitled to receive. We will also discuss the hammers and chisels that help chip away big chunks of royalties to which you would otherwise be entitled.

Royalties are defined, in part, as

> *payment made to a composer by an assignee*
> *or copyright holder for each unit or copy sold*
> *of the composer's work.*

When you sign an *Exclusive Songwriters Agreement* or a *Single Song Agreement* with a publisher, you are almost always giving up ownership of your song(s), or some portion thereof, as in the case of a *Copublishing Agreement*. In return, you get a portion of royalties collected in the event that song is recorded, released, and it earns money.

Performance Royalties

Under normal circumstances, ***performance royalties*** should be paid directly to you by your Performing Rights Organization (PRO), such as *BMI, ASCAP,* or *SESAC.* These royalties come from the use of your music in all performance situations, including radio and live music venues, among others. There are certain exceptions for some educational and religious uses. But, as many of you know, if you have a very successful hit song, the bulk of your royalty income may well come from performance royalties.

Other Royalty Income

The following is a list of other royalty-income sources from which the publisher pays the contractually agreed-upon percentage of royalties to you, the songwriter:

- ***Mechanical,*** which covers, CD, tape, and album sales;

- ***Sheet Music*** sales;

- ***Sync Licenses*** for synchronization of music to film, movie tapes, etc.;

- ***Background Music*** for elevators and similar uses;

- ***Special Licenses***--i.e., commercial, merchandising, etc.;

- *Grand or Dramatic Rights*;

- *Foreign royalties* which cover performance, mechanical, and other royalties earned in other countries; and

- *DART Royalties* from the use of digital hardware and software.

THE DART BILL

Until recently, the *Nashville Songwriters Association International (NSAI)* legislative effectiveness had been confined to *grassroots* efforts to stop legislation harmful to songwriters and copyright holders. Now, with the recent passage of the *Digital Audio Recording Technology (DART)* Act, NSAI has, for the first time, been able to assume the initiative by helping pass legislation to benefit those same parties.

DART legislation provides for a royalty on all digital blank tapes and a surcharge on every piece of digital hardware. This is not only a wonderful victory for the present, but a powerful precedent for all future digital technologies. Extensive discussions on the methods of collection and distribution of this *new royalty source* are in progress.

DART Background

Congress passed the precedent-setting legislation on October 7, 1992 as the *Audio Home Recording Act (AHRA)*, which was signed into law by President Bush on October 29, 1992. The AHRA, now known as the DART Act, will provide songwriters and music publishers, along with others in the industry, a percentage share of the sale of

- *digital software,* such as the blank Digital Audio Tape (DAT);

- *digital hardware,* such as DAT recorders; and

- any future *digital-related technologies* that may emerge.

Designed to reduce financial losses to the music industry from home taping, the law applies only to the *digital recording technology* which makes possible perfect copies of an original recorded work. The law does not apply to the currently used *analog recording technology* which has been generally available to consumers for years. The victory is the result of lobbying efforts that began some 3-plus years ago to prevent unregulated mass marketing of digital recording technology.

How It Will Work

Until DART, songwriters and other music creators had no means of receiving royalties on any of the creations recorded without permission. With DART, royalties on digital products are to be collected by the U.S. Copyright Office and deposited into two funds--a *sound recordings* fund and a *musical works* fund. The money in the two funds will be distributed to performers, composers, and other copyright holders, including music publishers and record companies whose audio works have been distributed to the public.

The total royalty pool will be allocated by the following percentages:

- *Record Companies* will receive 38.41 percent;

- *Featured Artists*, 25.60 percent;

- *Songwriters*, 16.66 percent;

- *Music Publishers*, 16.66 percent;

- *Musicians*, 1.75 percent; and

- *Background Vocalists*, 0.92 percent.

The law also requires manufacturers of digital audio equipment to install a serial copy-prevention system that will permit a copy to be made of an original recording, but would make it impossible to make a copy of the copy, thereby preventing unauthorized mass duplication.

As to *who* will *collect and distribute* any DART/DAT royalties in the future, the Performance Rights Organization(s), publishers, and private corporations, such as Copyright Management, Inc., have all thrown their hats into the ring!

This is the first time that royalty funds have been assigned specifically to songwriters. The songwriter should be aware that the *right to collect and distribute* these royalties does NOT belong to any group either by statute or by custom. This is a *NEW RIGHT*, and it is the songwriter's prerogative to assign it for collection wherever he/she chooses. And, since those who will *collect and distribute* will profit from the effort, this *new right* represents a clear opportunity for the songwriter to employ his/her prerogative as a possible bargaining chip.

Passage of the DART Act was made possible through the lobbying efforts of the music business *via* the Copyright Coalition, which included organizations such as the *National Music Publishers Association, Record Industry of America, ASCAP, BMI, NSAI, National Academy of Songwriters (NAS), Songwriters Guild of America*, and hardware manufacturers, among its membership. NSAI and NAS have since resigned from the Coalition.

The legislative battles that the Coalition will fight for protection under the copyright laws are far from over, but the passage of this bill is a great beginning.

DEDUCTIONS AND EXPENSES

It is obvious that not every dime of royalties collected is profit. There are many *deductions*, both legitimate and not so legitimate, that reduce the amount of your royalty check.

The following is a list of expenses that publishers incur in the normal course of business:

- *Overhead*.   This   includes   rent/mortgage,   office expenses, support personnel, etc.;

- *Royalty payments* to songwriters;

- *Copyright administration*;

- *Promotion*, which is defined as the

  advertising of a song to the general public to stimulate record sales, or independent promotion of a particular record to radio to stimulate airplay and eventually sale of the record.

- *Demo production*; and

- *Legal services.*

Not all of these expenses should be chargeable against *your* royalties. What should be charged against you are items like

- *your share of demo costs* if applicable;

- *advances*;

- *your share of collection fees*; and, occasionally,

- *a portion of independent promotion money if* you have agreed to the expense in advance.

Note that your fair share of *legal services* may be charged against royalties due you if they were incurred directly in connection with one of your songs. Usually, legal fees passed on to songwriters are related to the collection of royalties or to disputes concerning ownership or infringement actions. A publisher's general legal fees for advice on how to operate the company are part of the *cost of doing business* and should *not* be deducted from songwriter royalties or income. And, such items as *administrative overhead* are not your responsibility. (*CHAPTER VIII. ADVANCES AND RECOUPMENT*, p. 30).

The *ROYALTIES* section of your contract should include a definition of *gross receipts* and a definition of *net income*.

Read those definitions to determine the regular-basis deductions from your royalty check.

When dealing with a multinational publishing company, it is especially important to include a clause that specifically prevents the multinational publisher from ***double-dipping***-- i.e., charging a collection fee for monies collected in a foreign country and a collection fee on the same monies once received in the United States. Such a clause should read something like this:

> *The Publisher's share of amounts collected by the publisher's foreign music publishing subpublishers, which shall be calculated by them at the source, as received from them by performing and mechanical rights societies and other licensees, AND SHALL NOT BE REDUCED BY DISTRIBUTION BETWEEN VARIOUS UNITS OF THE MUSIC PUBLISHING GROUP, are deemed to be a percentage of the amounts actually received.*

This clause is a paraphrase of a clause appearing in a contract offered by a leading multinational publishing company. Pay particular attention to the caps. The publishing company has, to its credit, very pointedly agreed not to double-dip collection fees from both its domestic (US) and foreign subsidiaries.

The same publisher uses a ***net income clause*** which reduces gross receipts by

- an *administration fee* of 5 percent of the gross receipts;

- *copyright registration fees*;

- the costs of preparing *lead sheets and other administration expenses,* excluding overhead;

- *demo costs*, approved by both parties in writing; and

- actual and reasonable *out-of-pocket audit and litigation collection expenses*.

This *net income clause* is somewhat more detailed than that of other publishers who will often define net income only as *gross receipts less costs of collection.*

What works for you is up to you, your attorney, and your publisher. But, get *gross receipts* and *net income* or equivalent terms defined in your contract.

Foreign Collections Costs

You should also try to specify in your contract what *percentages are allowable for foreign collection.* Where the subpublisher is merely collecting royalties in the territory for records originally acquired by your publisher or you, a 10-percent collection fee would be a great deal. A more typical fee would be 15 percent and, at worst, 25 percent. If your publisher cannot or will not agree to a specified commitment in your contract--perhaps because publishers have different agreements in various territories--then, at least, negotiate for a *not-to-exceed* percentage of 25 percent.

When the subpublisher gets a *cover version* of your song in his/her territory, the subpublisher will usually receive a larger royalty percentage for this cover version. A typical percentage split will allow the subpublisher to keep 40 percent and to forward 60 percent to your publisher for accounting to you. The split may be 50-50 or 30-70. Again, you may want to specify a *not-to-exceed* percentage in your contract.

Sometimes a subpublisher will have a foreign translation done of the lyrics to your song, or will have an entirely new foreign lyric written to your melody. You definitely should *spell out in your contract whether this is permitted and, if so, how the foreign lyricist is to be compensated*. Over the years, songwriters have been robbed of royalties when a subpublisher listed the local songwriter(s) on a song by way of translation. Subsequently, the society of that territory also credited that songwriter and, therefore, that publisher with royalties earned by the English version.

If you permit translations, you should specify that the subpublisher

- must first make a specific request and get approval;

- is solely responsible for whether the translator is to be paid a flat fee for the work; and that

- in no case is a translator or new lyricist to receive more than a 10- to 15-percent royalty fee for that version.

The English language version can be differentiated from the foreign version by the *product* or *matrix number* which determines mechanical royalties. The lyricist's fee for performance royalties should be computed by the same ratio that the translated version represents to the original in mechanical royalties. Since many foreign societies distribute both mechanical and performance royalties, they are a central source for this information.

Free Goods

Another deduction of sorts that you need to be familiar with is *free goods*. Free goods is a contemporary and somewhat soulless term meaning *giveaways*. It brings to mind a phrase attributed to a famous record producer, *the product used to be called 'music,'* and he wished it still was!

Generally, publishers are paid for free goods although it often takes an audit to collect from the label. But, somewhere in your contract, your *publisher will reserve the right not to pay you on free goods*. If you are a songwriter with some clout, you may be able to put a ceiling on the amount of allowable free goods.

GETTING YOUR MONEY

Your publisher should distribute your share of royalties earned at least every 6 months, along with an accounting of where those royalties originated. Some of the more progressive publishers distribute on a quarterly basis. For the beginning songwriter, the publisher should split all royalties received on a 50-50 basis. Some publishers will give less on sheet music sales, folios, and the like.

As you develop a track record, the split may increase in your favor. The amount of increase depends on your relationship with your publisher, your publisher's bottom-line ability to pay and, sometimes, the ability and willingness of your attorney to negotiate. Extremely successful songwriters may move from a *Publishing* or *Copublishing Agreement* to a simple *Administration Agreement* in which the publisher charges a fee for administration and the songwriter retains copyright ownership and the vast majority of the royalties (*CHAPTER VII. ADMINISTRATION*, p. 25).

No matter what percentage you are receiving, there is a time lag between the date the publisher receives a check from various sources and the time those monies are distributed to the songwriters. Your publisher, as any good business person would, banks these large sums of money and collects interest on the *float* until it is time to pay you according to the terms of your contract. Publishers have been known to hold royalties for longer periods of time in order to benefit from the float. *So, be sure you are paid within 45 to 90 days after the accounting period in which your royalties were received.*

While the majority of publishers pay royalties to the songwriters on time, there are a few who hold back payments as long as possible. Occasionally, a publisher turns up that has not been paying songwriters any of the royalties earned and due. The best way for you to deal with these problems is to have a clause in your contract which requires a publisher to

> *pay on time or face a monetary penalty and/or forfeiture of copyright ownership.*

Further discussions on these situations appear in

- *CHAPTER XIV.* ***ACCOUNTING AND AUDIT***, Page 66;

- *CHAPTER XV.* ***OBLIGATIONS OF SONGWRITER AND PUBLISHER TO AN EXCLUSIVE SONGWRITERS AGREEMENT***, Page 72; and

- *CHAPTER XIX.* ***BREACH OF CONTRACT***, Page 93.

Should you face a situation where your publisher pays in an untimely fashion or has withheld royalties owed to you for whatever reason, please report it to the *Nashville Songwriters Association International*. Such conduct not only affects your fellow songwriters, but the entire music industry. Even if the publisher is not in breach of contract, he/she may be in breach of your personal trust. It is incumbent on us, as songwriters, to heighten our own awareness of both the benefits and the less redeeming qualities of our industry in order to improve it. ♪

X. THE CONTROLLED COMPOSITION CLAUSE

The Copyright Act of 1976 was the product of very difficult negotiations between the record labels and the music publishers. For the first time since 1909, the statutory rate for the **mechanical reproduction** of a song was increased from 2 cents to 2.75 cents. Since then, the rate has been increasing every two years to its current level of 6.61 cents.

Shortly after these increases came into effect, the record labels greatly expanded a practice requiring artists and producers to sign contracts containing a **controlled composition clause**, which is defined as

> a song written, owned, or controlled by an artist or producer, or in which either has an income interest.

The artist or producer is required to

> guarantee that controlled compositions will be licensed to the label on terms more

> *favorable than the terms of the typical mechanical license by publishers.*

The standard rate reduction asked is **75** percent of the statutory rate in effect on the date of the initial recording of the song. That reduced rate also remains frozen and is not affected by the biennial rate increases. The controlled composition clause is also used to limit the number of cuts paid on an album and to guarantee the record company a free rate on **cutouts, free goods**, etc.

What does this mean to the songwriter? For a **songwriter who is not an artist**, the effect can be felt if you cowrite with an artist. Some artists will extend the courtesy of asking the cowriters and the cowriters' publishers to **grant a rate** although, under the copyright law, the artist does not necessarily have to ask. It can be intimated that failure to grant a rate will result in dropping the song from the project, or not considering the song for a single. Many artists are not comfortable when they find themselves in this situation. They just absorb their cowriters' 25-percent reduction out of their artists' royalties. It is good to be aware of this before cowriting with an artist or a producer. As you go in, find out **whether you will be put in the position of having to grant a reduced rate**. The fact remains that the artist can just grant the reduced rate without asking.

For the **songwriter/artist**, it is important that the publisher insert into the *Exclusive Songwriters Agreement* a clause in which the songwriter agrees to use his best efforts to have the controlled composition clause **stricken** from his/her recording agreement. Failing that, however, the

> *publisher agrees to grant the license at a mechanical royalty rate of no less than 75 percent of the statutory rate then in effect.*

Needless to say, neither publishers nor songwriters are happy with this practice; but, there have been few breaches in the solidarity of the record labels on this issue. Labels may also waive the controlled composition clause or, at least, the reduced rate if the artist/writer signs with an affiliated publishing company. ♪

XI. EXISTING CATALOG

An ***existing catalog*** is a

> *collection of songs previously written and currently uncommitted to a publisher.*

If you are bringing an existing catalog into a new deal, you should expect to be compensated. This can be done in various ways.

- First of all, ***quantity and quality of songs*** will be taken into account by the publisher. For songs the publisher chooses to accept, a writer should try to obtain an ***outright purchase***. If the publisher refuses this and insists on a ***recoupable advance***, go for more money up front.

- Another option is taking no money up front, but asking for a ***larger advance for the term of the contract***.

- You may even ask for ***copublishing of songs*** in your existing catalog.

■ Also, you could even stipulate that the publisher may earn all or a portion of the copyright of a particular song in your catalog *if and when the publisher gets the song recorded*.

Several possible combinations of the suggestions listed above could be applicable to your existing catalog and would work well, depending on your situation and needs. If you have a better idea than any of these, *go for it*. ♪

XII. DEMOS

Your **demo** provides the suit of clothes your song will wear through the market place to attract attention; hence, its importance is never to be underestimated! Whether you are an entry-level or an advanced songwriter, the ultimate goal should be the same--i.e., **ownership, or some degree of ownership in the song and all business aspects associated with the song**. To this end, both entry-level and advanced songwriters should be shaping and examining these thoughts from the outset in any negotiation.

If you are an entry-level songwriter, some publishers will subject you to a subservient role regarding the demo process. Budget per song, recoupment, place of demo, producer of demo, and access and/or ownership of demo may well be fully controlled by your publisher. However, be aware that, **as your status as a songwriter improves, so should your voice and participation in the decision-making process**. Each aspect of the demo process should be thoroughly discussed and **anything agreed upon verbally should also appear in black and white**.

Both entry-level and advanced songwriters should consider the following questions with a prospective publisher:

- *Who has the last word as to whether or not a song is demoed?*

- *Is a **work tape** sufficient or is a **full demo** required to present the song properly? Again, who decides?*

- *Is the **demo budget** set in stone, or is there any latitude given on a per-song basis for special situations?*

- *Is the budget realistic?* The current average budget is $300 to $400 per song for a *typical* country song demo. For pop and other forms of music, demo budgets can be considerably higher.

- *Who pays when the demo goes over budget?* Common practice is for you and the publisher to split the *cost overrun*, but this will vary. The composer should also consider the budget limit a *protection* since the composer may pay for the entire excess or have it recouped from his/her royalties. Further, if the writer is not producing the demo session and does not approve the excess cost, the excess should not be recoupable from the writer. The excess should be charged against the party in control of the session and the expenses. At the least, *get a joint consent provision in your contract requiring both songwriter and publisher to agree on any averages*.

- *Who produces the demo?* The producer will, in all likelihood, determine the **configuration of the band**, select the **vocalist** for each song, and determine **when and where** the demo will take place. Joint approval or consultation with the songwriter is preferable.

  Some of you are apt to have your **own facility**. If that is the case, terms should be discussed as to **reimbursement** for whatever you provide--your **time, tape, and out-of-pocket expenses**.

- *Will you have the opportunity to* **reassess the demo** *of a given song for redemoing, remixing, resinging, and for rewrites?*

- *What happens to* **the 2-inch masters?** Some publishers make a mix of the demo tracks minus the vocalist then reuse the 2-inch tape for other demos. There are arguments for both saving and reusing the tape. Again, you are well advised to discover and discuss each aspect of this process.

- *If, at some point, the songs revert back to you, are the* **demo masters** *also included in the reversion?* This is often overlooked in *Copublishing Agreements*, and no provision is made for the writer/publisher to have access to or make copies of the demos.

- *Are there* **safety copies** *made of the demo masters which are kept at a separate location?* While this should be a standard procedure, it often is not. Make sure the publisher will *never* have the right to exploit the demo other than as *a demo*. This is especially important for writer/artists.

- *As a matter of course, do you receive a statement of demo costs with a breakdown of the costs per song within a reasonable amount of time following each demo?* You should always have an eye toward business. Your publisher most assuredly will, and you should do the same!

We *stress the importance* of thoroughly discussing with your publisher what will transpire once the pen is lifted and the song is declared complete. In negotiating your contract, we urge the use of unbridled imagination-- certainly, no less imagination than when writing your best song. You may not get all you want; but you will never get it unless you ask for it! But, as one attorney commented,

> *Always keep in mind that you are entering a partnership and not the boxing ring. So, don't leave too many scars from your negotiations. If possible, let your attorney be the 'bad cop' and you maintain a creative relationship with your publisher.*

For a discussion of publisher recoupment of demo costs, see *CHAPTER VIII. ADVANCES AND RECOUPMENT*, Page 30. ♪

XIII. CONSENT FOR COLLABORATION

According to a Nashville attorney,

> *Under the copyright law, any work - including a song - that is created by two or more persons 'with the intention that their contributions be merged' into a single unit is considered a 'joint work,' the ownership of which is shared by all of the contributors. Thus, unless there is some agreement to the contrary, the presumption is that each of the co-writers owns an undivided interest in the song, not simply his or her contribution to it.*

It's very simple. Write with people with whom you are comfortable cowriting. Good chemistry generally will yield a good song. But, if you consent to write with someone and then find the collaboration incompatible, you should *feel no obligation to continue the relationship.* Your publisher may suggest different collaborators for you to consider but, ultimately, the *area of consent should be yours.* In light of this, there is no reason for you to feel compelled to get written permission from your publisher to cowrite. We feel that all *written-permission requirements in contracts should be deleted!* Any such requirements are impediments to creativity!

A publisher's objection to a particular cowriting relationship may be because the cowriter and/or the cowriter's publisher may have neglected to pay shares of costs associated with the song that stemmed from the collaboration. It is much simpler to agree to discuss possible cowriters with your publisher. If your publisher objects to a specific cowriter, ask to know the reasons for his/her objections. They may well have merit and you may choose not to write with the prospective cowriter. ♪

XIV. ACCOUNTING AND AUDIT

ACCOUNTING

One of the responsibilities of publishing is handling the *money which is spent, advanced, or distributed; and that which is collected*. The songwriter who self-publishes may use minimal methods. But, when entering into a publishing contract with another party, the songwriter needs to pay careful attention to all the details involved in *accounting*.

While *record companies* typically account for royalties to publishers on a quarterly basis, most *publishers* account to songwriters on a *semiannual basis*. You may want to attempt to have your publisher account on a quarterly basis. The chances of being successful at acquiring this may be remote, particularly with a large publisher, but it is certainly worth trying to negotiate.

The typical semiannual periods end on June 30 and December 31. Then the publisher will have from 30 to 90 days after the close of the period to account to the songwriter. This means that a royalty dollar collected by the publisher on January 1 and credited to the songwriter on that date--i.e., the day after the close-of-accounting date--that royalty dollar will not be due and payable until a period usually between August 1 and September 30. This gives the publisher a considerable length of time to *use* the writer's money--i.e., collect interest on it, pay overhead, etc. In banking, this time period would be called the *float*-- i.e., the time between collecting money and having to pay it back out. Float is also discussed in *CHAPTER IX. ROYALTIES*, Page 40.

To offset this delay, songwriters often take an *advance* against future royalties. If used only as a means of *reversing the float*, an advance is very desirable. However, most often publishers make additional demands throughout various provisions of a contract when an advance, particularly a sizeable advance, is involved (*CHAPTER VIII. ADVANCES AND RECOUPMENT*, p. 30).

Accounting Statement

What should an **accounting statement** *provide*? Considering the sophistication of computers and software today, many publishers' statements are questionably Spartan. The basics are *the monies the publisher paid the songwriter in advances plus chargeable expenses against the monies credited or due to the songwriter from royalties received*. It is in your best interest to specify what should be contained on each statement through language in your contract. Ask for the following.

- *Date of issuance and amount for each advance.*

- *Date and specific explanation for each chargeable expense.* If demo costs are involved, the songwriter should require copies of contracts and receipts for musicians, studio, tape, etc., to document these charges. The contract should state that

    no such expenses are chargeable without such documentation.

- *Identification of the date, source, period reflected, and percentage credited for royalties shown.* Copies of source documents for all royalties should be available upon request.

- *Periodic statements from the publisher*, regardless of whether or not a payment is due.

AUDITING

In fairness, accounting at a large publishing company is a complex matter. Hundreds, sometimes thousands of writers and copublishers must be paid accurately from sources around the world. This makes the *audit* provisions of the songwriter's contract extremely important. The typical publishing contract tries to limit severely the songwriter's ability to audit.

The songwriter must be prepared to negotiate hard in this area. A songwriter should not settle for anything less than the following regarding rights of auditing the publisher.

- *Two years minimum in which to audit* from the date the statement was issued. This can represent almost a 3-year period if the statement reflects monies collected 9 months before. A time period of 3 to 5 years would be better still. Ideally, no time period would be imposed.

- *Notify the publisher with a written notice* 1 week prior to auditing. Some contracts try to stipulate 30 days or more--a delaying tactic.

- *Impose no restriction on the specifics of the audit.* Believe it or not, some contracts provide that the

    songwriter must inform the publisher, in writing, what is being questioned specifically,

    and restrict the scope of the audit to that one item; or, impose a restriction that the

    songwriter is only allowed one specific audit on any given statement;

    or, require that the

> *auditor chosen by the songwriter to represent him/her may not represent any other songwriter affiliated with that publisher;*

or, require that the

> *auditor be a CPA;*

or, impose a

> *time limit on the length of the audit.*

All of these restrictions, along with any other handcuffing foolishness, *should be removed from your contract if possible*.

- *If an error is found which is greater than a specified percentage*--e.g., 5 to 10 percent--the publisher should correct the error and pay interest at a designated rate on that amount. If such an excessive error is discovered, the contract might also stipulate that the

  > *publisher should pay the cost of the audit.*

- *Request timely statements*. Although it will be difficult to achieve, a songwriter should attempt to add language to the contract specifying that the *songwriter's commitment to perform is contingent on the timely receipt of statements, not to exceed 3 months beyond the statement due date, with interest accruing during that time.*

Receipt of the statement should be a condition precedent to the songwriter's further performance under the contract. Should the publisher fail within that period to account properly, then the ***copyrights should revert to the songwriter and the contract should be terminated***. ♪

XV. OBLIGATIONS OF SONGWRITER AND PUBLISHER TO AN EXCLUSIVE SONGWRITERS AGREEMENT

PUBLISHER'S OBLIGATIONS

A careful review of a customary *Exclusive Songwriters Agreement* will reveal surprisingly few obligations to be undertaken by the publisher. The publisher is generally required to **pay some sort of advance** to the songwriter, provided the songwriter chooses to take one, and to **account to the songwriter for mechanical or other royalties** owed to the songwriter. But, in terms of exploiting the songwriter's material, a publisher is usually only required, if at all, to use **reasonable efforts** (*CHAPTER XIX. BREACH OF CONTRACT*, p. 93). Further, the publisher generally has the power to deem whether or not any song is **commercially acceptable** and to decide, without consulting the songwriter, whether or not the song is **exploitable**.

For these reasons, it is most important for you, the songwriter, to investigate a publisher before signing an agreement to insure that the publisher is willing and able to work hard on your behalf. For instance, try to find out if the publisher is willing to

- set you up with other accomplished songwriters and artists,

- provide constructive criticism of your work, and

- help promote your career, in general.

It is imperative that you **look into the publishing company's reputation and standing in the music community**. A good way to validate the publisher's track record and overall ability is to talk with other songwriters who have been or are with the publishing company at present. If it is a new company that has potential, then a song-by-song agreement with a reversion clause or a *Copublishing Agreement* with similar terms might be more suitable to you. Either way, all agreements and commitments should be confirmed in writing.

Additionally, it is important to remember that each situation is unique and some tradeoffs may have to be made, depending on the songwriter's needs and the willingness of the publisher to meet them, or *vice versa*. For instance, if you need a large advance to cover personal overhead, you may wish to sign with a *major* publisher and sacrifice some of the personal attention a smaller publisher would be able to give.

We strongly recommend that you take the time to read *CHAPTER XIX.* *BREACH OF CONTRACT*, Page 93. It discusses the current, somewhat lopsided, state of *Exclusive Songwriters Agreements*, and offers some important suggestions for contractual clauses which will encourage your publisher to work harder for you and to make your publisher more accountable for his/her actions.

SONGWRITER'S OBLIGATIONS

In an *Exclusive Songwriters Agreement*, the songwriter is primarily obligated to **create songs** which may be recorded either by the songwriter or by another artist; and, whether the songwriter is writing alone or cowriting, it is his/her responsibility to get the job done.

Songwriting is a job and should be treated accordingly. But, how you accomplish your work depends on your relationship with your publisher, and an *Exclusive Songwriters Agreement* helps to define that relationship. Since all agreements are unique, a variety of obligations may be considered, depending on the circumstances surrounding the deal. Consider the following.

- *Quota for songs*. A publisher may require you to produce a specific amount of songs in a year's time-- e.g., 12 wholly written songs per year. Generally, quotas are set up on a whole-song basis--i.e., a song written alone is considered **1** whole song applied toward the quota. A song written with one cowriter would normally apply as **1/2** of a song toward the quota. *Be sure your contract addresses this issue* to prevent any possible misunderstandings between you and your publisher in the future. This is especially true for songs that have three or more cowriters.

- *Originality of work.* In every songwriter contract, there is a clause in which you *guarantee* that the songs you write are not ripoffs of someone else's work. If you are committing artistic theft or are plagiarizing, you are responsible for the consequences (*CHAPTER XVII. INDEMNIFICATION FOR LAWSUITS*, p. 85).

- *Commitment to write on site at publisher's premises.* If a publisher has a facility with writers' rooms, then the songwriter may be required to write at the *office*. If the office is open from 9 to 5, then the publisher may ask songwriters to come in during that time. But quality writing time varies from songwriter to songwriter, and such parameters and time limits may be counterproductive. *Be sure all time commitments are clearly defined in the contract.* In the event that the management of the publishing company changes, there will be no question as to what is expected if terms are well spelled out. Again, compare your situation with other songwriters.

- *Obtaining publishing rights from unsigned cowriters*. Some publishers will require you to use *reasonable efforts* or *best efforts* to have an unsigned cowriter assign his/her interest in a song over to your publisher. This requirement varies from publisher to publisher and you should *be sure you understand what your publisher's policy is and what your contract requires of you*. Applied practically, your reasonable or best efforts probably means that you will ask your cowriter if he/she is willing to give up ownership interest in the song, nothing more.

- *Procedures for cowriting*. Some publishers may require you to write with songwriters selected by your publisher or may require you to write a certain number of songs with other *in-house* writers. This may or may not be a healthy situation. A lot depends on your relationship with your publisher. Talk it over with other songwriters and *compare your publisher's requirement to the requirements of other publishers before you sign*; but, especially talk it over with *other signed songwriters of that publishing company*.

- *Getting written permission to cowrite*. Such a requirement is not generally acceptable. If your publisher tells you that he/she never enforces the clause, then tell him/her *that's all the more reason to get it out of your contract.* For example, if you neglect to secure written permission to cowrite and your relationship with your publisher deteriorates, it could come back to haunt you in a number of ways. It could subject you to a **breach-of-contract claim** by your publisher. Also refer to *CHAPTER XIII. CONSENT FOR COLLABORATION*, Page 64. ♪

XVI. LIMITATIONS OF PUBLISHER'S USE OF COPYRIGHT

When you enter into an *Exclusive Songwriters Agreement* or *Single Song Agreement* with a publisher, you **should not be giving him/her the right to do anything they want with your song**. You have rights, too. It is, after all, a partnership you are about to enter into. There are certain **limitations** that you may want the publisher to observe concerning your work. A publisher should **never** allow the following without your consent in writing.

- **Fundamental changes in your song**. No one should be allowed to change the lyric, melody, or title without your approval, except when translating it into a foreign language (*CHAPTER IX. ROYALTIES*, p. 40).

- **Mechanical licenses for less than the statutory rate**. There is a great deal of controversy over this one, especially when cowriting with an artist whose contract states that the artist must grant a reduced rate on any of the songs that he/she has written and recorded. **Get the right to say 'no' to a reduced rate in your contract,** *then follow your conscience.* (See *CHAPTER X. CONTROLLED COMPOSITION CLAUSE*, p. 55.)

- *Use of your song in a film, television, or commercial.* You might not want your song used in beer commercials, political commercials, or in ways to which you object on principle (*CHAPTER I. MORAL RIGHTS*, p. 2).

- *Dramatic interpretation of your song.* In a way, this restriction falls under the preceding one, above; but, it also covers live theatrical performances and, in this day and age, videos.

- *Use of your name and likeness, such as photographs.* This is not really a copyright issue, but *it is* a contractual issue. Most of the time, your publisher will want you to give him/her the right to use a likeness of you to promote your songs. Just get it *in writing that it must be a picture you have approved*.

All of the above are only precautionary guidelines to follow while you *read that contract before your hand is on the signature line*.

Bottom line?

- *You need to have the right to authorize every use of your music just in case there is some incident you cannot foresee.* At least, require your publisher to consult with you prior to making changes.

79

- ***Under no condition should changes be made which result in division of royalties without your prior approval.*** You never know what new technologies might come along and change the face of the licensing of copyrighted music. Cover your bases.

- One last item. Usually there is some clause that gives the publisher the right to authorize various activities in your behalf if you cannot be reached, like when you are on Mars or in a coma! In these days of portable intergalactic personal-information fax-o-telephonic data devices that are the size of thumbtacks, ***there is really no good excuse for your publisher not to be able to find you.*** So, ***eliminate the authorization clause.***

Finally, be reasonable. If someone wants to pay you a truckload of money for the use of your song in a commercial selling a deodorant that you do not like, talk it over with your publisher. ***Make a responsible business decision.*** It may be worth accepting the money offer. ♪

XVII. RIGHT OF TRANSFER/ASSIGNMENT

Traditionally, a clause appears in an *Exclusive Songwriters Agreement* which allows the publishing company to transfer its interests in the copyrights to your songs and its interests in your exclusive services as a songwriter to a third party-- usually, to another publisher. But you, the songwriter, are not free to transfer your interests in the contract to another party. That only makes sense since the **publisher signed you for *your* ability to write songs, and you cannot transfer that ability to someone else**.

Still, the proposition that your publisher could sell your contract and your songs to another party may be unsettling. *Why?* You could have signed with your publisher because there are 4 songpluggers servicing 12 writers and a catalog of 1000 songs. One day your publisher wakes up and decides he/she is tired of dealing with all of you and **sells the catalogs and songwriters' contracts to a big corporation** where no one is responsible for anything, there are

4 songpluggers to service 80 songwriters and a catalog of 30,000 songs. . . You just may not want to be there.

So, how do you get out of it? **If your transfer/assignment clause is typical, you may not be able to get out of your deal on any legal basis.** Your only choice may be to ask your way out. If you are successful, your future obligation to write songs for the publisher may be terminated. However, songs already written usually go along with the songs in the catalog which is sold.

You may have a couple of contractual options if you have the clout and foresight to have them included in your contract:

- **Key-Man Clause.** If you sign with a publisher because you particularly like a songplugger or the owner of the company or whomever, you may have your attorney insert a clause, provided your publisher is willing. The clause may state that

    if that particular songplugger leaves the company, you have the option of terminating your agreement at that time.

- **Right to Terminate in the event of sale of company or catalog.** This is self-explanatory. You may ask for a clause which states that

> *in the event the publisher sells the catalog or the company, you have the right to terminate your Exclusive Songwriters Agreement with the publisher.*

In either this case or in the case of the **Key-Man Clause**, above, you may not be able to take songs you have written during the term of your *Exclusive Songwriters Agreement*, but you may be free to look elsewhere for a new publisher suitable to your needs.

■ ***Notice of Intent by the publisher to sell you and your catalog.*** See if you can get a clause which requires your publisher to

> *inform you, in writing, at least 30 to 60 days prior to the closure of sale of the catalog that the publisher is, indeed, selling your catalog.*

Insert a provision which

> *imposes some sort of penalty such as liquidated damages--i.e., a specific amount of money--on the publisher for failure to notify you per the terms of the* **Transfer/Assignment Clause** *that you and your songs are being sold to another publisher.*

The **Key-Man Clause** currently appears, from time to time, in *Exclusive Songwriters Agreements*. The second and third items in the above list are, at best, rare. That does not mean you cannot try to get them included now or at some later date. ♪

XVIII. INDEMNIFICATION FOR LAWSUITS

INDEMNIFICATION CLAUSES

Assume that one of your songs has become a smash hit. You and your publisher are thrilled until, out of the blue, someone comes forward and claims that the song infringes on the copyright of another song. *What to do?* The typical music publishing agreement, be it a *Single Song Contract* or an *Exclusive Songwriters Agreement*, contains provisions that anticipate this unhappy event. Contracts that fail to address this possibility should be avoided.

These provisions often contain language similar to the following excerpt related to *indemnification clauses*.

> *In the event of the assertion of any claim by a third party, which is inconsistent with any of the warranties, representations, covenants, or agreements made by Songwriter in this Agreement, including, without limitation, a claim that the Composition infringes upon any*

> *other composition, Publisher shall promptly serve notice of such claim upon Songwriter and Songwriter may, at his sole cost and expense, participate in the defense of any such claim. Publisher shall have the right to control the defense thereof and to settle or otherwise dispose of such claim in any manner which Publisher, in his/her sole discretion, may determine.*

This language, in essence, puts the publisher in the driver's seat when defending against any claim or lawsuit concerning the song which typically would be based on alleged copyright infringement. Such a claim often takes the form of a letter from the claimant to the publisher, and may be received months or even years before a lawsuit is eventually filed. Under the quoted language, although you would have the option to share the costs incurred in the defense against such a claim, the **publisher** has the **sole** right to make all the decisions on whether to

- fight it out in court, or

- simply pay to settle the matter.

At the least, you should try to **negotiate for this right** if it is absent from the contract presented to you. In fact, you might prefer to negotiate for a provision that would allow you to

*have an equal say with the publisher over
whether such a claim should be fought or
settled.*

The publisher, in turn, might agree to this provision only if
you further agreed to share **up front** in the cost of any court
battle.

Alternatively, you might propose a provision allowing you
to

*take over the expense and control of a lawsuit
if you think it is better to refuse a settlement
that your publisher believes to be reasonable.*

Such disagreement between songwriter and publisher is not
unheard of. For example, although a settlement might
appear to be financially reasonable from the publisher's
standpoint because the claimant is willing to settle and **go
away** in exchange of a small payment, the settlement might
be unacceptable from the songwriter's standpoint if it
appears to be an admission that he/she stole someone
else's song.

HOLD-HARMLESS CLAUSES

*Composer agrees to pay and indemnify and
hold harmless Publisher for any loss, damage,
judgment, award, cost, or expense, including*

> *reasonable attorneys' fees, incurred or paid by*
> *Publisher in connection with or related to such*
> *claim.*

This is called a **Hold-Harmless Clause**, by which one person (in this case, the composer) agrees to reimburse another person (in this case, the publisher) for losses and/or to absolve the second person from responsibility. Under the quoted language,

> *you agree to reimburse the publisher for ANY*
> *AND ALL money that the publisher ultimately*
> *would have to pay if someone made a claim*
> *against the song.*

This would include not only the amount of a judgment in a lawsuit but, theoretically, every penny of defense costs spent by the publisher from the date of the claim, including office expenses and attorneys' fees. Significantly, the quoted language **requires you to reimburse the publisher for those amounts** even if the claim ends up being an utter sham and infringement is never proven.

Although it would be reasonable for you to foot the bill if infringement has occurred, it is **unclear why you should reimburse the publisher for all costs of defending against a meritless claim** just because some crackpot may have decided that his/her lyrics were telepathically stolen from a dusty lockbox in the attic. Instead, you might want to negotiate for a provision that, *as a legitimate risk of doing business, the publisher will at least bear half the expense if the claim ultimately proves to be without merit.*

Moreover, you might try to negotiate for a provision stating that the

publisher agrees to indemnify **you** *for any claims stemming from his/her activities.*

Consider it a precautionary measure.

CROSS-COLLATERALIZATION CLAUSE

In addition to any other remedy of Publisher, and notwithstanding any other provision hereof, until any such claim has been adjudicated or settled, Publisher may withhold any and all monies due and payable to Composer under this or any other agreements between the parties hereto. Upon final adjudication or settlement of any such claim, such monies may, at Publisher's option and to the extent necessary, be applied in satisfaction of such judgment or settlement and/or Publisher's loss or damages arising therefrom.

This is called a *Cross-Collateralization Clause*. Under the quoted language, if a claim is made against the song, the publisher can withhold your royalties to apply toward any costs, not only for the song in question, but also for any other songs of yours that are with the publisher. In the worst case scenario, a claim might be made against a relatively unsuccessful song, for which the publisher would have the right to withhold all of the songwriter's royalties, including those in the *pipeline*, for an extremely successful song that is totally unrelated to the claim. *The songwriter's entire royalty income on all songs with the publisher could be held indefinitely until the claim is resolved*.

For that reason, you should consider negotiating the following variations to such a provision.

■ It would be preferable for the publisher to agree that,

> *if a claim is made against a song, the publisher can only withhold royalties due on that song.*

■ It would be preferable for the publisher to

> *agree to a limit on the amount of money that the publisher could withhold while a claim is pending.*

For example, it would be reasonable for the publisher to agree that the royalties withheld not exceed an amount necessary to satisfy the claim and indemnify the publisher. This amount may be difficult to determine, given the fact that the amount demanded might well exceed any reasonable recovery.

■ It would be reasonable to require the publisher to

place any withheld money in an interest-bearing escrow account on behalf of the writer while the claim is pending.

■ You might negotiate for a limit on the length of time that the publisher can withhold royalties. For example, such a provision might state that,

if no lawsuit is brought within one year after the claim was first made, then the withheld money will be released to the songwriter.

■ You may request a provision that offers some security to the publisher and states that,

if you are able to post a mutually agreeable surety bond, then no royalty payments will be withheld while the claim is pending.

In this situation, you might pay a premium to a bonding company which, in turn, would agree to reimburse the publisher's costs in defending against the claim if you, for some reason, failed to do so.

Although this might sound like a good idea to a songwriter who prefers to keep royalty income flowing while a claim is being resolved, in reality it might be difficult to find a bonding company that would charge a reasonable premium for such an arrangement unless you have sufficient other assets to secure the obligation to the bonding company. ♪

XIX. BREACH OF CONTRACT

We found early on in this endeavor that, in all contracts, the songwriter's duties and responsibilities were invariably laid out in detail and always in accessible language. There is never any doubt when the **songwriter is in breach of contract.** However, because of prevailing attitudes and, because of the way songwriter deals are written, **rarely is a publisher found to have breached a contract**. Aside from nonpayment of royalties, suspension of a songwriter's advance, and dissolution and/or bankruptcy of the publishing company--and not always in these cases--the publisher resides in a redoubt of time-honored tradition and, for the most part, appears to be above reproach.

It is important to emphasize that **we strongly feel that songwriter-publisher relations should, at no time, be adversarial, but should always strive toward partnership.** Further, we submit that the adversarial language employed in the drawing of contracts to govern these relationships perpetuates confusion and division and ultimately may serve far better the legal profession which draws the instruments than it may serve you, the songwriter, and your prospective publisher.

As indicated in several of the preceding chapters, the purpose of this handbook is to equip the songwriter with information regarding areas of songwriter-publisher relationships which deserve closer scrutiny. In this chapter, commentaries will deal with contract changes recommended as necessary if the songwriter is ever to achieve some type of parity in the relationship.

What follows, then, is a discussion of certain points that we have deemed problematic. These points may, in fact, stem from obtuse legal language in all contracts and may cause formidable difficulty for the songwriter down the road if they are left unchallenged.

UNIQUE SERVICES CLAUSE

The current *Unique Services Clause* may be considered a weapon handed the publisher to move against the songwriter (*CHAPTER I. MORAL RIGHTS*, p. 2). Suppose the songwriter quits writing, or acquires a horrendous writer's block. This little gem enables the publisher to enjoin or prevent the songwriter from going to another publisher. There are, however, no similar means that the songwriter can use contractually to force the publisher to do anything aside from allowing the songwriter to conduct an audit of royalties and other income received by the publisher.

Under the current arrangement, songwriter contracts are better likened to indentured servitude! For this to change, we believe that, in all songwriter contracts, there must be clauses detailing the *mutual responsibilities* of both parties and the attending consequences should either party fail to perform. For too long, the publisher has hidden behind a smokescreen of confounding legalese and has shrunk from any accountability.

It is herewith noted that, when you fail to perform, you lose your gig and the publisher keeps the catalog. When the publisher fails to perform, you lose your gig and the publisher keeps the catalog! What is wrong with this picture? We suggest that you reread the preceding remark, and take a moment to think long and hard about what you have read.

FIDUCIARY RESPONSIBILITY

Although the law in this area is unsettled, some courts around the country have held that publishers may, in some instances, have a *fiduciary responsibility* vis-à-vis the songwriter. A young songwriter recently observed that the word *fiduciary* is much too big a word not to have any meaning. His comment piqued our interest. So, we consulted *Black's Law Dictionary*. It defines *fiduciary,* in part, as

> . . . . *The nature of a trust.* Moreover, a person is a fiduciary who is *invested with rights and powers to be exercised for the benefit of another person.*

95

It further states that a *fiduciary relationship* is one

> *subsisting between two persons in regards to a business, or a contract . . . of such a character that each must repose trust and confidence in the other and must exercise a corresponding degree of fairness and good faith.*

This all seems fairly clear; *but, alas, how does it apply in the songwriter-publisher relationship?* Here is what we believe. When you assign ownership of your copyrights to a publisher, you do so with the understanding that your publisher--as stated in your contract--will, in turn, pay you an agreed-upon percentage of royalties earned. You are entrusting your publisher with your copyrights and trusting your publisher to pay you later when the money comes in. That should create a fiduciary or greater-than-average responsibility which your publisher has to you.

Here is the problem. *What happens if you do not get paid? What recourse do you have?* Chances are your contract does not address that *at all*. And, when your publisher says, *'So, sue me,'* do you have the money to do it?

When a songwriter agrees to write to the best of his/her ability, the language and penalties are clear! But, when a publisher agrees to publish and conceivably owe a fiduciary responsibility to the songwriter and his/her work, there is rarely any clear definition of what happens if your publisher fails to exercise that responsibility.

Now, let us take it a step further. If you entrust your copyrights to the hands of a publisher, the fundamental reason you are doing so is to get cuts so that you can get paid... so that you can make a living. *Right? Shouldn't working your catalog be part of your publisher's responsibility to you?* We think so. But you will not see that acknowledged in your contract--at least, not beyond the use of the term **reasonable efforts**, which is discussed below. In fact, in most current contracts, what a fiduciary responsibility means remains a part of a nebulous body of thought to which only the legal gods are privy!

SONGWRITER-PUBLISHER CONTRACT CLAUSES PROPOSED FOR NEGOTIATION

While the songwriter hungers for specifics as to the publisher's duties and answerabilities, he is promptly served up a liberal helping of **reasonable efforts** and **best efforts.** *What's reasonable? What's a best effort?* The hour has arrived when both entry- and advanced-level songwriters should look for specific best efforts from publishers worth their salt, and should eagerly ask that the specific **best-effort** yardstick be applied to their own endeavor. To this end, we offer the following as a starter list of specifics that might be broached in future contract negotiations. At the very least, it is incumbent on you, the songwriter, to inquire as to your proposed publisher's policies and attitudes toward these matters **prior** to signing your contract.

- **Daily communication.** The particulars--i.e., the when, where, to whom--of each song pitch should be available to the songwriter. All responses, good or bad that are garnered in the pitching of that song should also be available, as should details regarding followups.

- **Songwriter participation.** The publisher should encourage the songwriter's participation in whatever way he/she can be utilized, such as making contacts, pitches, and so forth.

- **Publishers should be asked to commit to songs.** If publishers commit to a song, then they should pitch the song. We recognize that songs, even the best ones, are often not cut for years, with pitches running into the hundreds. So, it may take time. But, if the publisher is not willing to commit to the song by demoing and pitching it, the song should revert to the songwriter after some period of time--i.e., from **immediately to 3 years**, depending on what you negotiate. We believe the publisher should be accountable for more than the banking function. The major publisher today may be cutting into his/her catalog as many as 65 to 75 new songs each week. This means that a song is **new** for 1 or 2 weeks and then lost in a creative deluge. **Something must change in the realm of a publisher's commitment to work the songs he/she receives!**

- **Road support.** If a songwriter is asked to write with an artist on the road, airfare and accommodations should be readily provided. The cost incurred may be charged back to the songwriter's account, unless the travel is done at the publisher's request, and the publisher's willingness to provide such support should be a given. In any event, such arrangements should be mutually agreed upon in advance. At worst, settle only for a 50-50 split of expenses.

■ *The publisher should commit to raise the songwriter's profile at every opportunity.* Basically, this means that the publisher should always commit to pitch the songwriter and not merely his songs! This point may be difficult to state contractually. So, do your homework. Find out your prospective publisher's track record in this regard before you sign the deal.

■ *Publisher's bankruptcy.* There are war stories floating all around about publishers who go bankrupt, leaving catalogs stranded in the midst of lawyers, creditors, and trustees. Sometimes these catalogs are lost forever. A clause should be inserted in each and every *Exclusive Songwriters Agreement* or *Single Song Agreement* which states that,

> *if the publisher files bankruptcy, then all copyrights assigned to the publisher by the songwriter, as part of the agreement, should revert to the songwriter.*

This should be a *mandatory clause* for any contract entered into. You may face a hurdle enforcing the clause, depending on what other creditors are involved in your publisher's bankruptcy and on what the bankruptcy court has to say about it. But the clause still may give you an edge.

- *Get a security interest in royalties owed.* If you do not know what a *security interest* is, do not feel alone. It is revolutionary to songwriter-publisher agreements. The term *security interest* means

    a property required by contract to secure payments or the performance of an obligation.

It also serves to help prevent loss.

So, how does this apply to a song? It may be *your best protection* if your publisher refuses to pay you or if your publisher goes bankrupt. Ask your attorney to explain this option in detail and to tell you how it applies to you.

From a practical standpoint, getting a publisher to go along with signing a *security interest* is another matter altogether. But, now is a good time to start. Do not let your publisher tell you, it would be a paperwork nightmare. It is no more trouble than signing the short-form copyright assignment which your publisher requires you to do. Security-interest formalities do require a filing fee and the paperwork must be filed at the U.S. Copyright Office, along with the short-form assignment.

The foregoing list of possible contract inclusions is but a beginning. Still it serves notice to the songwriting community as to what is being omitted in the songwriting contracts; and, indeed, by omission, what is being foisted upon the songwriter through such innocuous phrases as *reasonable efforts* or *best efforts*, *fiduciary*, and *unique services*. ♪

APPENDIX A

ABOUT THE
NSAI EQUITY COMMITTEE MEMBERS

LEWIS ANDERSON, Cochair, NSAI Equity Committee, is a former *BMI Country Songwriter of the Year*, an active Writer and Publisher, as well as an A&R Consultant to MCA Records in Nashville. He is the recipient of an *NSAI Achievement Award* and the *NSAI President's Award* for creating the Professional Membership Division's *ProPosition* publication. Lewis' No. 1 songs include B. J. Thomas' "Whatever Happened To Old Fashioned Love," T. G. Sheppard's "Somewhere Down The Line," and Conway Twitty's "Lost In The Feeling."

DENNIS LORD also cochairs the NSAI Equity Committee, and serves as a Member of the NSAI Board of Directors. Dennis has the distinction of being both a Songwriter and an Attorney specializing in Entertainment Law; an Adjunct Professor teaching Copyright Law and Recording Industry Courses at Middle Tennessee State University; and a Writer at Bluewater Music. Dennis cowrote the Travis Tritt classic "Country Club."

MICHAEL CLARK writes at Warner/Chappell Music. He is a former Capitol Recording Artist and a former Member of NSAI's Awards Committee. Michael's songwriting credits include Alabama's "Reckless," The Oak Ridge Boys' "Come On In" and "True Heart," and The Pointer Sisters'/Conway Twitty's "Slow Hand."

STEVE DEAN writes for Tom Collins Music. Steve's songwriting credits include four No. 1 songs, Alabama's "Southern Star," Reba McEntire's "Walk On," The Oak Ridge Boys' "It Takes A Little Rain," and Lee Greenwood's "Hearts Aren't Made To Break." Some other singles are Steve Wariner's "Don't Your Mem'ry Ever Sleep At Night," Barbara Mandrell's "Fast Lanes And Country Roads," and Conway Twitty's "One Bridge I Didn't Burn."

GENE NELSON is a North Carolina native who spent several years writing and singing in Los Angeles before moving to Nashville in 1984. He is the Writer of three No. 1 hits, Doug Stone's "A Jukebox With A Country Song," plus Kathy Mattea's "Burning Old Memories," and "Eighteen Wheels And A Dozen Roses," a song that was named *1988 Song And Single Of The Year* by the Academy of Country Music, and the *1988 Single Of The Year* by the Country Music Association.

LISA PALAS is an NSAI Vice President, Chair of NSAI's Compensation Committee, Member of NSAI's Awards Committee, and serves on ASCAP's Southern Writers Advisory Board. Lisa's songwriting credits include a pair of No. 1 songs for Alabama, "There's No Way" and "(You've Got) The Touch;" and songs for The Whites' "Love Won't Wait," and The Shooters' "They Only Come Out At Night."

WILL ROBINSON. In addition to participating in the songwriters/publishers lobby against the DAT Bill in Congress, Will also has served on the NSAI Legislative Committee and on the CMA Special Events Committee. He has had an eight-year writing career with Maypop Music. Currently, he writes for Disney Music. Will's songwriting credits include the No. 1 singles, Doug Stone's "I Never Knew Love," Reba McEntire's "I Know How He Feels," Earl Thomas Conley's "What I'd Say," and Alabama's "There's No Way," "The Touch," and "Pass It On Down."

JIM ROONEY. A former Talent Coordinator of the Newport Folk Festival, Jim also managed Bearsville Sound Studios in Woodstock, New York, and was a Charter Member of the Woodstock Mountain Revue. In 1976, he moved to Nashville, where he later began engineering and producing artists such as John Prine, Jerry Jeff Walker, and Townes Van Zandt. Jim is a Partner in Forerunner Music Group and is Coproducer of Hal Ketchum, Nanci Griffith, and Iris DeMent. He also serves on the NSAI Pro Calling Committee.

JIM RUSHING. A Texas native, Jim is a former NSAI Board Member whose songwriting credits include Garth Brooks' "American Honky-Tonk Bar Association," Martina McBride's "Cheap Whiskey," Kathy Mattea's "Lonesome Standard Time," and Ricky Skaggs' "Heartbreak Hurricane," "Thanks Again," and "Cajun Moon."

KAREN STALEY. Karen is a Pennsylvania native whose apprenticeship has run the gamut of the music experience, from demo singing to touring as background vocalist and guitar player for Reba McEntire. She is the Writer of the Michael Martin Murphy & Holly Dunn No. 1, "A Face In The Crowd," which also was nominated for a *Grammy.* Karen's songwriting credits also include Rick Trevino's "Just Enuff Rope," Confederate Railroad's "She Took It Like A Man," Tracy Byrd's "Keeper Of The Stars," and Faith Hill's "Take Me As I Am."

INDEX

INDEX

A

Accounting, viii, 23, 26, 27, 50, 52, 53, 66-71
    for Monies, 27
    Semiannual, 66
    Statement, 67
Accounting and Audit, 66-71
Administration, viii, 10, 22, 25-29, 46, 49, 52
    expenses, 49
Administration, 25-29
Advance(s), 12, 14, 22, 23, 24, 26, 29, 30-39, 47, 58, 66, 67, 68,
    72, 93, 99
Advances and Recoupment, 30-39
Agent(s), 27
    for Collection, 26
    Exclusive, 26
Agreement(s), xi, xii, 1, 5, 6, 7, 10, 25, 27, 28, 37, 39, 50, 64,
    73, 74, 82, 85, 89, 99, 100
Agreement(s)
    Administration, 26, 27, 28, 29, 52
    Copublishing, 14, 21-24, 40, 52, 58, 62, 73
    Exclusive Songwriters, 9, 12, 21, 34, 36, 40, 56, 72-77, 78,
        81, 82, 83, 84, 85, 99
    Publishing, xi, xii, 1, 5, 6, 7, 12, 52, 72, 85
    Recording, 57
    Single Song, 9, 21, 40, 73, 78, 85, 99

I

J

L

M

N

O

R